THE  OF PATCHES
a Yiddish Folktale

adapted by Cynthia Burres
illustrated by Nancy Cote

Harcourt
SCHOOL PUBLISHERS

Printed in China

ISBN 10: 0-15-350672-5
ISBN 13: 978-0-15-350672-7

Ordering Options
ISBN 10: 0-15-350600-8 (Grade 3 On-Level Collection)
ISBN 13: 978-0-15-350600-0 (Grade 3 On-Level Collection)
ISBN 10: 0-15-357890-4 (package of 5)
ISBN 13: 978-0-15-357890-8 (package of 5)

11 12 13 14 15 0940 12 11 10

Once there was a man named Khaim Yankl. He lived with his family in a small hut on the edge of the woods.

It had not rained much that summer, and farmers could not grow food, so famine swept across the land. The family was in terrible trouble.

"I can't let my wife and six children starve!" worried Khaim. Finally, he determined that he had to take a desperate step.

Khaim calmly sat down with his family. "I'm a good worker, and I can do any job," he said. "However, there are no jobs available here, so I'm going out into the world. I will travel far and wide, and I will accept any job that pays even a penny. When I return, I promise that I will be rich. We will all have fine clothes, and we'll live in an enormous house. We will enjoy a banquet every night."

Khaim set out the next morning, taking nothing but the coat he wore. He walked and walked for many miles until he reached another village. Khaim went to every house, and he asked whether there was any work for him. There was none. Finally, when he reached the last house, he knocked on the door and a man answered.

"Excuse me, sir," Khaim said. "I need work. Is there anything you need?"

"Can you dig a well?" replied the man.
"Absolutely!" said Khaim confidently.

Khaim worked all day, and when he finished, the man was extremely generous. He paid Khaim with silver coins. Khaim knew he had to be careful because he could lose the money or be robbed. Suddenly, he had a fantastic idea.

Khaim hurried into town, changed his coins into paper money, and placed the money inside his coat. Then he sewed a patch over it so that no one could see the money.

Meanwhile, Khaim kept walking, and at each village, he made a little more money. Each time he sewed the money into his coat. He worked for years until the coat was completely covered with patches. Khaim was rich, and at last, it was time to return home.

One day, a man in a patched coat knocked on the family's door. They did not recognize him at first, but then his wife cried out in joy because Khaim was home at last.

"I have returned with plenty of money, and now I'm going to town to buy food for a delicious feast," Khaim declared. Khaim also had decided to buy a new coat, so he threw the old patched one onto the floor and left.

Then the family heard another knock. It was a poor traveler, asking for food. Khaim's wife gave him a loaf of bread and some cheese— after all, who knows how many people had helped Khaim as he wandered?

She saw the old patched coat lying on the floor and gave that to the poor man, too. Khaim could buy a much nicer coat now anyway.

Khaim returned, wearing a beautiful new coat. Now it was time to cut the money out of the old one.

"Where is my patched coat?" Khaim asked.

"Oh, that old thing?" shrugged his wife. "I gave it to a poor traveler."

Khaim fainted. When he came to, he cried, "I must get that coat back!"

Khaim ran all the way back to town, found a store, and bought a fiddle. Then he took the fiddle, and wearing his fancy new coat, he marched around the town, playing and singing at the top of his lungs. People came to the doors of their houses and shops to find out what all the noise was about.

"I'm a fool! I'm a fool!" sang Khaim. He marched to the village square, where a crowd gathered and stared with curiosity.

Some in the crowd recognized him. They noticed his fine coat as well as his strange actions. People whispered that at long last Khaim had made his fortune. He had returned home, but he was obviously not well.

Khaim began to dance in a silly way as he continued to shout, "I'm a fool!" However, all the while, he kept his eye on the crowd. Finally, his gaze fell on what he had hoped to see—the poor traveler, wearing the coat of patches.

Khaim marched over to the man and grabbed his hand. Khaim dragged him into the middle of the square.

Khaim put down the fiddle and took off his coat. He twirled the coat in a circle over his head so that everyone could admire the fine silk lining and the silver buttons.

Then he shouted, "Let's trade coats!"

The crowd gasped in horror. Why would anyone trade that beautiful new coat for the old patched one?

The poor man was certain that Khaim
was playing a trick on him, but Khaim kept
insisting. Finally, the poor man was agreeable.
He traded coats with Khaim. Then the man
ran off before Khaim could change his mind.
Khaim put on the old patched coat and danced
away from the square.

The crowd also drifted away. They shook
their heads sadly. Surely this must be proof that
Khaim was not well. It was indeed a sad sight.

Khaim raced back home, took off the old coat, and carefully began to cut the patches open. When he had cut open all the patches, Khaim picked up the coat and shook it with all his might. Money began to fall out of the patches.

The family gasped, and then they began to laugh. Now they understood why he'd wanted the coat back!

"I'm not a fool," winked Khaim. His family agreed, and they all lived happily ever after.

Think Critically

1. What is the main idea of the story?

2. How would you describe Khaim?

3. Why does Khaim change the silver coins into paper money?

4. How does Khaim feel when he finds out the patched coat is gone?

5. What do you think of Khaim's decision to leave his family to go find work?

 **Social Studies**

Look at a Map This story takes place in Eastern Europe. Look at a map or a globe of the world and write down the names of some countries that are in Eastern Europe.

School-Home Connection Look around your home. Is there anything you have that you wouldn't trade for anything in the world? Write a short paragraph that tells why it is important to you.